BACKYARD WITCH

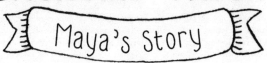

Maya's Story

by Christine Heppermann and Ron Koertge

illustrated by Deborah Marcero

Greenwillow Books, *An Imprint of* HarperCollins *Publishers*

Backyard Witch: Maya's Story
Text copyright © 2017 by Christine Heppermann and Ron Koertge;
illustrations copyright © 2017 by Deborah Marcero
All rights reserved. No part of this book may be used or reproduced in any manner whatsoever without written permission except in the case of brief quotations embodied in critical articles and reviews. Printed in the United States of America. For information address HarperCollins Children's Books, a division of HarperCollins Publishers, 195 Broadway, New York, NY 10007.
www.harpercollinschildrens.com
The text of this book is set in Berling Roman. Book design by Sylvie Le Floc'h

Library of Congress Cataloging-in-Publication Data
Names: Heppermann, Christine, author. | Koertge, Ronald, author. | Marcero, Deborah, illustrator.
Title: Maya's story / by Christine Heppermann and Ron Koertge ; illustrated by Deborah Marcero.
Description: First edition. | New York, NY : Greenwillow Books, an imprint of HarperCollins Publishers, [2017] | Series: Backyard witch ; 3 | Summary: When Maya, who has been preparing for the school spelling bee for weeks, loses to Sadie, Ms. M the witch appears to help Maya deal with her jealousy and learn to be a good friend.
Identifiers: LCCN 2016038272 | ISBN 9780062338440 (trade ed.)
Subjects: | CYAC: Friendship—Fiction. | Witches—Fiction. | Jealousy—Fiction. | Spelling bees—Fiction. | BISAC: JUVENILE FICTION / Fantasy & Magic. | JUVENILE FICTION / Social Issues / Friendship. | JUVENILE FICTION / Imagination & Play.
Classification: LCC PZ7.1.H47 May 2017 | DDC [Fic]—dc23 LC record available at https://lccn.loc.gov/2016038272

17 18 19 20 21 CG/LSCH 10 9 8 7 6 5 4 3 2 1
First Edition

 Greenwillow Books

*For my sister, Ann,
and her invisible chicken,
both uniquely inspirational birds*—C. H.

*For my wife, Bianca, and her invisible
kitten, which has her eye on Ann's
chicken*—R. K.

*For Danette,
my very first best friend* —D. M.

Contents

CHAPTER 1: Intergalactic Spelling Champion 1

CHAPTER 2: Unbelievable 11

CHAPTER 3: Now You've Done It 20

CHAPTER 4: The Substitute Librarian 28

CHAPTER 5: Spontaneous Psychic Activity 37

CHAPTER 6: Making a Snow Angel 52

CHAPTER 7: A Possible Explanation 67

CHAPTER 8: Bookhenge 81

CHAPTER 9: Emerald on the Inside 95

CHAPTER 10: Not a Game for Babies 109

CHAPTER 11: Imaginary Eggs 122

CHAPTER 12: Thanks for the Help 136

CHAPTER 13: One Codfish and Two Sharks 145

CHAPTER 14: C-e-l-e-b-r-a-t-e 156

Quiz: What's Haunting You? 175

Fun with Mnemonics, by Ms. M 183

Chapter 1

Intergalactic Spelling Champion

"Unstoppable," said Jess.

Maya didn't hesitate. "U-n-s-t-o-p-p-a-b-l-e." Like she would be tomorrow.

"Marvelous," said Sadie.

"M-a-r-v-e-l-o-u-s." Exactly how she would feel tomorrow.

"I have a great word," said Jess. "O-u-t-d-o-o-r-s. As in, let's get out of your boring basement and go outdoors." She vaulted from the flowered couch, where she had been sitting beside Sadie, and stretched her arms over her head.

"Too easy," Maya declared. She spelled it backward.

"Now I'm really dizzy." Sadie flung her copy of the practice list onto the rug. "I can't read anymore. My eyeballs are spinning." She got up from the couch, too. "I vote for a break."

Maya didn't budge from her beanbag chair. "We can't take a break. There are barely"— she squinted over at the clock on the cable TV box—"twenty-three hours and fourteen minutes left before the spelling bee."

"I don't know why you're nervous," said

Jess. She crumpled her copy of the list into a ball, tossed the ball in the air, caught it on the laces of her sneaker, catapulted it almost to the ceiling, and let it drop into her outstretched hand. "You win every year."

"True, but you know fourth grade is different. It's not just us. It's the fifth graders, too. And if I win—"

"*When* you win," Sadie said.

Maya smiled at her and continued, "When I win, I get to move on to the district bee. I'll be competing against the best spellers from every school."

Jess pretended to shoot a basket with the ball, sinking the shot into Maya's lap. "You'd win anywhere. Against anybody. If Martians had a spelling bee, you'd go to Mars and beat

them." Jess folded her arms across her chest. "When's the last time you got less than a hundred percent on a spelling test?"

Okay, it was true. Maya had always loved school. She was the best speller in her class, in her grade, in all of Piper Creek Elementary, probably. Now she had the chance to be the best in the city, and after that, who knows— the state, the country, the universe?

Maya Russell, Intergalactic Spelling Champion. She pictured herself holding an enormous trophy that reflected the sun.

"Look, Jess." Maya tried a different approach. "You're really good at sports, but I would never tell you to skip practice before a tournament. And, Sadie, I'd never tell you to stop learning about birds."

"I still have a lot to learn about birds," Sadie pointed out. "You haven't missed a word all afternoon."

Maya uncrumpled the balled-up list and smoothed it against her leg. "Just a little while

ms. m

longer, okay? We can at least be as diligent as Ms. M."

"Ms. M," said Jess. "I wonder if she found Ethel?"

Ms. M was their friend. She was also a witch. That made her extra-fun to be around. Except they hadn't seen her for a while. She had gone off to search for her best friend, Ethel, who—here it gets complicated—had accidentally turned herself into a bird. A yellow warbler, to be exact.

"If Ms. M hasn't found her yet, she will," Maya assured Jess. "She's d-i-l-i-g-e-n-t."

Just then Maya's mother appeared on the stairs in her police uniform. "I'm off to protect and serve. Your father's responsible for feeding you." She blew a kiss in Maya's direction.

"Oh, and be patient with your brothers."

"They're not coming down here, are they?" Maya whined. As if on cue, Victor and Barnabas clattered past their mother. Actually, only Victor clattered. He wore cowboy boots. Barefoot Barnabas thumped from step to step like a giant rabbit.

"Oh no." Maya sat up taller in the beanbag chair. "They can play in their room. Or the yard. Or Alaska."

Her mother laughed. "Honey, they've been waiting all weekend to play with their Lego village. You've been working hard. Go get some fresh air." She left the basement door open on her way out.

The twins stepped carefully into the Lego village and began to build.

"What are you guys making?" asked Sadie, squatting down next to Victor.

"A barn for Caitlyn," said Barnabas.

"Who is Caitlyn?"

Maya groaned. "Don't encourage him!"

"Shhh!" Barnabas brought his finger to his lips. "Caitlyn's sleeping. Over there." He pointed to a pile of laundry in front of the washing machine in the corner.

"Caitlyn is his imaginary chicken," Maya explained wearily.

Barnabas cocked his head toward the corner. "She's awake now. And she says *you're* imaginary. You just don't know it."

"So," said Jess, rocking back and forth on her heels. "Are we out of here, or what?"

"Twenty more words first," Maya said.

Jess looked at Sadie. Sadie looked at Jess. They shook their heads in unison.

"Fifteen more words?"

"Maximus wants to go outside with you," said Victor as he snapped a section of roof into place.

"I bet I'm going to be sorry I asked this," Jess said. "But who is Maximus?"

"I-m-a-g-i-n-a-r-y," said Maya. Then she added, "Ten more words."

"Maximus is my friend," Victor told Jess. "He likes you. A lot."

"I was right," said Jess. "I am sorry. Last one to the swing set is a rotten tomato!"

T-o-m-a-t-o, Maya thought as she chased her two best friends up the stairs.

Chapter 2

Unbelievable

The next morning, Maya stood onstage looking out at all the faces in the Piper Creek Elementary School auditorium. She felt a little seasick. All those eyes focused right on her!

She wiped one slightly sweaty hand against the other, cleared her throat, stepped forward to the microphone, and said, "Somersault. S-o-m-e-r-s-a-u-l-t."

Ms. Boswell, the assistant principal, tapped the little bell that meant correct. *Ping!* From

somewhere in the audience, Jess whooped.

The crowd onstage shrank. It was like a mystery story where everyone vanished one by one.

Alicia fell to *vertebrate*.

Cameron misheard *morale*.

Khalil conquered *catastrophe* but stumbled over *obstruction*.

Ms. Boswell showered positive comments like "Good job!" and "Tough break!" on the eliminated spellers as they trudged to their seats. She beamed rays of encouragement at the four spellers left.

At the three spellers left.

At the two.

At Maya and Sadie.

Sadie. Unbelievable.

Every time Sadie stepped up to the microphone for her turn, she looked terrified, as if she were walking the plank on a pirate ship. She quivered through *mystify*, clutching the end of her long dark ponytail so hard that wisps of hair fluttered from her fingers when she let go. Maya wanted to rush over and give her a hug. Instead, as she passed by Sadie on her way to the microphone, she sent a telepathic friend message: *Don't worry. This will all be over soon.*

Maya attacked *havoc*.

Sadie sighed before *finagle*.

Maya sailed through *suspicion*.

Sadie tangled with *meander*.

Maya demolished *dilemma*.

Sadie paused in the middle of *abundant* . . .

". . . a-n-t?"

Ping!

Out in the audience, some boys made a commotion. Ms. Boswell turned around and transformed her ray of encouragement into a laser of disapproval. "I know we've all been sitting for a long time, but please continue to give our two amazing spellers your full attention." She turned back. "Ready, Maya?"

Maya nodded into the microphone.

"Ornithology." *It means the study of birds,* Maya thought, glancing quickly at Sadie.

She cleared her throat. Vowels and consonants swirled around her. She waited for them to settle into a well-behaved row. Except this time they just kept circling like raptors, refusing to land.

"O," she began. Hesitated. "R." Frowned.

More rumpus from the middle of the room.

"Gentlemen!" Ms. Boswell snapped.

Flustered, Maya spelled quickly. "O-r-n-a-t-h-o-l-o-g-y."

There was no *ping!* Only silence.

A silence that meant WRONG.

From the front row, Jess gaped up at her, openmouthed.

A wave of disbelief followed by a tsunami of humiliation washed over Maya as she stepped back from the microphone. But if Sadie spelled the word wrong, too, the competition would continue. So she still had a chance.

"Ornithology," Sadie repeated. "O-r-n . . ." She stopped. "Can I start again?"

Ms. Boswell nodded.

Maya sent another telepathic message: *Come on, Sadie. Hurry up and miss.*

"O-r-n-i . . ."

Maya held her breath.

"O-r-n-i-t-h-o-l-o-g-y?"

Ping!

Any moment now, this horrible dream would be over. Maya pinched her arm to wake herself up.

Instead the cheers and applause only got louder.

In the dream, Ms. Boswell climbed the stage steps and presented the silver trophy shaped like a cheerful bumblebee to a stunned-looking Sadie. Then she turned and held out a limp red ribbon. "And congratulations to you, too, Maya."

Wake up, wake up, wake up! This isn't happening!

Maya took the ribbon. She stared down at the printed gold letters that spelled out her worst nightmare:

S-E-C-O-N-D P-L-A-C-E

Chapter 3
Now You've Done It

"This is my worst nightmare!" Sadie howled.

Mr. Frederick stopped the line of fourth graders on their way back to class after the bee. "Pipe down, please, Room 142."

Once the line started moving again, Sadie continued in a softer voice, "I have to compete in the district spelling bee, and it's all Maya's fault!"

"What do you mean?" Maya forced herself to say the awful words: "*You* won. Not me."

"I wasn't a good speller," Sadie explained, "until you made me help you practice. And now I'm doomed."

"You could get sick," said Jess. "Maya's the alternate. If you're sick, you stay home, and she goes in your place. Everybody wins."

Maya walked a little behind Sadie and Jess, concentrating on the floor with its checkerboard pattern. She wanted to jump from one black square to another until she was out of this school, out of this city, and in the forest, where she would live with animals who didn't talk, much less spell.

Sadie slowed almost to a stop and tried to hand her trophy to Maya. "You deserve this.

I couldn't help knowing *ornithology*. It's in practically every birding book I've ever read. Why didn't I just miss on purpose?"

"Don't worry." Maya looked at her friend. "The district bee isn't for three whole weeks. You have lots of time to study."

Sadie shook her head vigorously. "Jess is right. I'm totally getting sick. Did you hear Darren sneezing during math? I'm going to thumb-wrestle him and steal his germs. Hold this."

Reluctantly, Maya took the trophy. Her fingerprints smudged the smooth plastic base, still warm from the heat of Sadie's hands. The cheerful bumblebee smiled up at her.

As Sadie hurried toward the front of the line to talk to Darren, Jess shook her head. "Colds don't last three weeks."

"She could eat the chicken fingers at lunch and try for typhoid."

Now the bumblebee's smile looked a little off-kilter. Almost sarcastic. *You hope Sadie catches a serious illness? Wow, Maya. You're such a great friend.*

They reached the doorway to their classroom. While Jess and Maya waited for everyone ahead of them to file in, Jess said, "Remember last spring when I went to take that perfect shot on goal, and my cleat flew off and hit Midori in the head? I didn't score, we lost the game, *and* I almost gave our best striker a concussion."

"Just that game," Maya pointed out. "You still won the championship." The bee's smile seemed judgmental. *Don't be a baby! She's*

Don't be a baby!

just trying to make you feel better.

Mr. Frederick clapped his hands. "All right, people, let's get cracking. I want your erosion charts turned in by the end of class."

Sadie stood hunched by the pencil sharpener with Darren, their thumbs locked in combat. Maya walked toward the back of the room to put the trophy on Sadie's desk. But when she got there, she couldn't seem to let go.

Nice knowing you. The bee smirked.

Maya stroked the bee's smooth round stomach. Tugged at the little black ball atop one of its springy antennae.

How does it feel to play second fiddle? the bee sneered.

Maya tugged at the ball harder.

Why don't we look at your prize? The bee aimed a withering glance at Maya's skirt pocket. The pocket that held her pitiful ribbon.

Maya tugged so hard that . . .

The antenna came off!

Ouch! Now you've done it. You're in big trouble.

The tears rolled. She couldn't stop them.

"Maya?" Beside her, Mr. Frederick's voice

rang with concern. *Wait till he sees what you've done.*

"I—" The antenna dangled from her hand. "I didn't mean to. I'm sorry."

"Why don't you head down to the library until lunch?" As Mr. Frederick took the trophy and antenna away from her, the bee flashed a triumphant grin. *Guilty!*

"It's not a punishment," Mr. Frederick explained. "The substitute librarian looked a bit . . ." He scratched his shiny bald head, as if searching for the word. "Frazzled this morning. I told her I'd send a student to help out. A responsible student."

Responsible. R-e-s- . . . NO.

Out loud, she said, "What about my erosion chart?"

Mr. Frederick smiled gently. "Take it home and finish it tonight."

On her way to the door, she passed Sadie, who pantomimed blowing her nose.

Gross, Maya thought. And unnecessary. Because Maya wasn't going to be the alternate.

In fact, she was n-e-v-e-r going to spell again. Starting now.

Chapter 4
The Substitute Librarian

Maya dawdled in the hall. The slower she walked, the less time she would have to spend in the library, surrounded by books. Books filled with words. Thousands of pages of words. All taunting her. All daring her to try and spell them.

Music spilled through the open doorway

of the kindergarten classroom. There was Ms. Shaw, strumming her guitar, leading her students in a song about the days of the week.

If only Maya could go back to kindergarten, where things were easy! Where she'd earned smiley-face stickers just for knowing that Tuesday comes before Wednesday, or for tying her shoes.

As she passed Mrs. Delgado's first-grade classroom, she glanced inside and saw Barnabas over by the terrarium, talking to his friend James. Or, rather, James was talking. Barnabas was listening. And frowning. And fuming. Yikes. He was about to explode. But before Maya could catch his eye, he stomped out of sight.

Finally, unavoidably, she reached the door to the library. Except it didn't *sound* like the library. What a racket!

On the story carpet in front of the puppet theater, a class of second graders giggled and shrieked and bopped one another over the head with cushions from the reading nook. Where was the substitute librarian?

Just then, from behind the puppet theater, came a blast of kazoo-like trumpets followed by an announcement. "And now, the original version of 'Cinderella'!"

That voice sounds so familiar, Maya thought as she took a seat on the floor at the back of the rug.

The red curtains parted to reveal a witch

puppet with green hands and a green face. She waved to the audience. A few second graders waved back. Others simply stared.

A prince wearing a gold cape and crown popped onto the stage. He bowed to the witch and held out a tiny slipper. "If this fits, we'll get married and live happily ever after."

The second graders looked at one another. "No," a girl in denim overalls objected. "That's the end of the story."

"The end is my favorite part," said the witch puppet. "That's why I always eat dessert first."

"And there's no witch in 'Cinderella,'" the girl said.

"There used to be. Before those gloomy Grimm brothers got hold of it. In a very early version, the prince danced all night with an attractive young witch. I'm not saying it was

me, but I'm not saying it wasn't."

"Tell us a real story!" demanded a red-haired boy sitting in front of Maya.

The witch puppet rested her green hands beneath her pointy chin. "Hmmm. All right, here's one of my favorites."

Down went the prince, and up came a princess with long, curly black hair. She wore a yellow dress with puffy blue sleeves. "Look what a nice lady just gave me," said the princess, holding out a red apple the size of a jelly bean.

With a wicked forehand, the witch knocked the tiny apple nearly across the room, making three students duck. "Never accept fruit from a stranger!"

"If that's supposed to be Snow White, where

are the dwarves?" asked a girl kneeling in the middle of the audience, hands on her hips.

"Stuck in traffic," said the witch puppet.

The red-haired boy started clapping slowly and chanting, "Real story. Real story. Real story." Other kids joined him.

This was getting out of control. Maya leaped to her feet. "Hey, you guys, settle down. Give her a chance."

The red-haired boy glared. "You're not our teacher."

"No, but I am," called Mrs. Zhang, who had, thankfully, just appeared in the doorway. "And much as I hate to cut this, uh, creative retelling short, it's time to get back to class. Second graders, line up quietly, please."

"Come by tomorrow," said the witch,

waving. "I'm doing 'The Enchantress and the Beanstalk.'"

That voice. That raspy, friendly voice. The more Maya heard it, the more she was sure.

The witch puppet disappeared below the stage as the children, jostling one another and whispering, followed their teacher out.

"Ms. M?" Maya called out in the now-empty library. "Is that you?"

Chapter 5

Spontaneous Psychic Activity

The red curtains seemed to shimmy. And then a real witch stepped out from behind the puppet theater. She had a pointy hat, but she wasn't green. She was as tall as Maya. She had a warm, snaggletoothed smile.

"Maya, dear," said Ms. M. "So lovely to see you."

Incredible! "What are you doing here? I thought you went home to look for Ethel."

Ms. M stepped closer. For the first time Maya noticed that the witch's eyes were brown, the same as her own. "Alas, I was too late," the witch said. "I found beak

PUPPET

marks in my butter, but no Ethel."

Ms. M started tidying the cushions, picking them up one at a time and flinging them like Frisbees into the reading corner.

Maya joined in. After a moment, she asked, "How did Ethel get into your house?"

"Ethel's my best friend." Ms. M sent an orange cushion soaring. "Of course I gave her a spare key."

"How does a bird carry a key?" asked Maya, genuinely curious.

"Briefly, if I know Ethel. She loses everything." Ms. M smoothed her black smock dress and straightened her black pointy hat. "I'm just glad to know she was there. Though I do wish she had left a note."

"And you're here in the library because ...?"

"I'm filling in for Mrs. Gardiner while she's on medical leave."

"So you've worked in a library before?"

"Libraries are some of my favorite places, but the real question is, do I have experience with spontaneous psychic activity?"

Spontaneous. Before Maya could stop them, the letters began to assemble in her mind. *S-p-o-* . . . *NO!*

She shook her head to clear it. "I'm not sure what spontaneous psychic activity has to do with—"

"Here, let me give you a demonstration." The witch squatted down by a low shelf labeled EARLY READERS. She moved half a dozen books to the floor. Then from the shelf she pulled a volume that stood a little taller and thicker than the rest. "Look."

Maya read the title out loud. "*The Encyclopedia of Plant Life.*"

"Exactly. And where does it belong?"

Maya didn't hesitate. "Shelved with juvenile nonfiction. Or maybe reference."

The witch nodded so enthusiastically her hat swayed. "And yet we find it here. In early readers. What does that suggest to you?"

Maya shrugged. "Somebody put it in the wrong place, I guess."

"Somebody." Ms. M scooted close enough so that Maya breathed in her familiar dusty, cinnamony smell. "Or no body."

"I don't get it."

"All I'm saying is, our culprit may lack material form."

"Oh!" Maya suddenly understood. "You mean, a ghost!"

Ms. M nodded and sat back on her heels. The pointy toes of her shoes curled against the carpet. "I witnessed a disturbance much like this once. At a bookstore in Düsseldorf. The poltergeist there was equally fond of disorder."

"A poltergeist?" Tough to spell—not that Maya was tempted—and even tougher to believe.

Ms. M explained, "*Poltergeist* means 'noisy ghost' in German. Which could be devastating in this particular setting. Our ghost seems to be the quiet type so far." She set *The Encyclopedia of Plant Life* neatly on top of the stack of books and then added, "Exhibit One."

Maya tried appealing to reason. "But, Ms. M, it's just a mis-shelved book."

"Exhibit Two." She pulled *The Very Hungry Caterpillar* from the stack. "This didn't just crawl over to the middle-grade-fiction section all by itself." With the book she pointed toward the puppet theater. "Exhibit Three. When I came in this morning, the hand puppets were neatly laid out. Yet when I went behind the curtain to do story time, they were all jumbled up."

"And you think that means the library is haunted by a noisy ghost who's the quiet type? I'm not sure I—"

Maya was interrupted by two fifth-grade boys, Otto and Jason, bursting into the library. Otto had "Skate and Destroy" scrawled on his T-shirt in Magic Marker. A series of fading skull tattoos marched down Jason's right arm.

"Where's Mrs. Gardiner?" Jason asked Maya.

Ms. M rose slowly to her feet. "The permanent librarian is home recovering from elbow surgery. In the meantime, my assistant and I are at your service."

Assistant, Maya thought, standing up a little straighter. *With three S's separated only by an* I. Not that it mattered anymore.

Otto gawked at Ms. M. "Why are you dressed like that? It's not Halloween."

Ms. M smiled at him. "You're right, but thank you for reminding me to start planning my costume. Last year I couldn't decide whether I wanted to be a firefly or a firefighter. I finally went as both. Red suspenders. Rubber boots. Gossamer wings and a battery pack so my backside lit up."

Jason snorted. "Are you sure you're a librarian? Because you sure don't sound like one."

Maya stepped forward. "For your information, Jason, Ms. M is a witch. For real."

Jason looked Ms. M up and down and smirked. "Sure she is."

"All day, every day!" Ms. M said brightly. "Now let's concentrate on your reason for being here, which is—" She narrowed her eyes, turned both palms toward the ceiling, and muttered under her breath. Next she used one hand to tilt her hat this way and that, as if adjusting an antenna. Finally she said, "Egypt. Eighteenth dynasty. Am I right?"

Otto's mouth fell open. Jason mumbled, "Wow, yeah. Mummies and stuff. How did—"

Ms. M stepped away, retrieved her voluminous black bag from under her desk, and plunked it down on the nearest table. "You're in luck. Not only is this library a trove of Egyptian lore, I believe I have some actual platypus. As you know, the ancient Egyptians wrote everything on platypus."

"Uh, Ms. M?" Maya adopted a level, lukewarm tone. "I think you mean papyrus."

"I might mean a lot of things." Ms. M opened her bag, waved away a small cloud of smoke, and plunged in one arm. The bag bulged here, then there, then somewhere else. "Sorry," the witch murmured. "Go back to sleep." In a louder voice, she said to the boys, "Let's see what we have here." The witch's arm disappeared into the bag again.

Everyone leaned forward as Ms. M pulled out a small trowel, a dusty wide-brimmed hat, safety glasses, a battered notebook, two

small brushes, and finally—"Aha!"—a scroll of very old-looking, very thin, very yellow paper with tattered edges. She carefully unrolled one of the outer leaves to reveal dim, mysterious writing.

"Hieroglyphics!" shouted Otto.

The witch put on the safety glasses, picked up a brush, and carefully swept sand away from the scroll. "I haven't read this in a while, but I believe it says, 'Pick up some barley and watch out for crocodiles.'"

"Can I touch it?" Jason said breathlessly, peering at the brittle page.

"Of course." Ms. M began putting everything away in her black bag. Almost everything. After rerolling the scroll, she handed it to Jason. "And if you promise to be careful, you can use it for your project."

"This is too cool, Ms. M," he said. "Thanks a lot."

Once the boys left, Maya turned to Ms. M, who was now humming and swaying back and forth with her bag cradled in both arms.

"You don't actually have a platypus in there, do you?" Maya asked.

The witch stopped humming and pressed a gnarled finger against her lips in a *shhh* gesture. "Maya, you know the platypus is a semi-aquatic mammal. I have a lot of things in my bag, but a pond is not one of them." She bent down and gently stowed the bag back beneath her desk.

Maya eyed the big, round clock on the back wall. "I'm supposed to go to lunch now.

Will you be okay on your own?"

Ms. M straightened. "Certainly, dear. We'll continue our investigation into paranormal activity tomorrow."

"That sounds great, but I don't think Mr. Frederick will let me come here every day."

"He will," said Ms. M with a mischievous grin. "Leave it to me."

Uh-oh. "Mr. Frederick is nice. Please don't put a spell on him. He likes being human."

"Not a spell. Donuts. He told me in the teachers' lounge that chocolate glazed are his favorite."

Maya laughed. "Well, okay then. See you tomorrow."

Heading toward the cafeteria, Maya felt lighter than she had since . . . well, who needed a cheap plastic trophy? She had Ms. M.

Sadie and Jess would be thrilled that the witch was back! That she was right here at school!

Wait.

Sadie and Ms. M were good friends. In fact, for a while Ms. M had lived in Sadie's backyard playhouse.

Jess and Ms. M were good friends. In fact, Ms. M had been Jess's babysitter.

Maya had never had Ms. M all to herself. Until today. Especially today, when she could use a friend who was interested in noisy ghosts, not spelling bees.

Chapter 6
Making a Snow Angel

Back in the classroom after recess, Maya was baffled. Where had the bee trophy gone? Had Mr. Frederick fixed it?

More important, did Sadie know Maya was the one who had broken it? And if she did, was she mad? She didn't seem mad at lunch, but maybe she was just waiting to confront Maya later.

Maya didn't feel like finding out.

When the final bell rang, she grabbed her things from her cubby faster than usual and sped off without waiting for her friends.

Outside, kids swirled every which way, like confetti. She spotted her dad's minivan in the pickup circle and headed straight for it.

"You're here early." Her father smiled as she yanked open the door.

Barnabas and Victor were already strapped into their booster seats, muttering to each other in some secret twin language that only Ms. M might understand. Maya dropped her backpack onto the floor and tried to squeeze between her twin brothers.

"That's Caitlyn's place!" Barnabas objected.

"Would you like somebody to sit on you?"

"I can't sit on a chicken that doesn't exist," Maya said under her breath. Not far enough under, apparently, because Barnabas pulled her hair.

"Hey! Stop!"

"I don't care what anybody says," Barnabas fumed. "Caitlyn's right there. You see her, don't you, Victor?"

"Yep," said Victor, making it two against

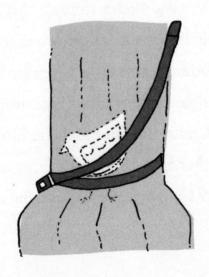

one. As usual. "You better watch out, Maya. She's mad. She could peck your eyes out."

Maya appealed to her father. "Dad, please make these children behave!"

Victor made a face at her. "You're children, too."

"We're not going anywhere," her father cut in, "until *everyone* settles down. Children and chickens. Maya, sit in the way-back, please. More room there, anyway."

As her father pulled the minivan away from the curb, Maya grumbled, "I'm not sitting on Maximus now, am I, Victor?"

Victor shook his head. "He took the bus. With Jess. He's going to give her a friendship ring. She'll show it to you tomorrow, probably."

Had she been that peculiar when she was

in first grade? No way. She'd had real friends. Sadie and Jess.

And look how well that turned out.

At least imaginary friends couldn't beat you in spelling bees.

As if her dad could read minds, he caught her eye in the rearview mirror. "So where's that trophy from the spelling bee? Is it big and shiny? Does it have your name on it already?"

Maya turned to stare out the window. Leaves shook in the breeze, as if the trees were laughing. A flock of geese flew overhead in perfect V formation. *Show-offs*.

"Maya?" her father asked. "Where's the—"

"Caitlyn says the trophy is invisible," Barnabas interrupted with a smirk. "And anyway, Maya didn't win."

Her father negotiated a tricky roundabout with a dry fountain in the middle. "But you studied so hard. What happened?"

"She came in second," said Victor. "Maximus won."

Maya gritted her teeth. "He did not. Sadie won, Dad. And not me."

"I see. Well, I'm sorry, honey," her father said. "But look at it this way. When Willie Mays was batting over three hundred, he missed about two-thirds of the time. So you had some bad luck. You'll get 'em next time."

"Thanks, Dad, but spelling isn't like

baseball. You don't get three strikes. Miss one word and you're out. For a whole year."

Victor piped up, "Barnabas got in trouble today."

Maya's father gave a low whistle. "Mama's not going to be happy about that. What's the story, B?"

Barnabas kicked the booster seat as he explained. "James and Fernando hurt Caitlyn's feelings (*kick*) because they said she's not real (*kick*) and she wanted to get away from them (*kick*) so I had to open a window so she could fly outside (*kick*) and Mrs. Delgado got mad at me (*kick*) even though it was all (*kick*) James and Fernando's fault." (*Kick, kick, kick, kick, kick, kick, kick, kick . . .*)

"Barnabas! Enough."

"He had to clean up after we had raisins and carrot sticks for a snack," Victor added. "Tomorrow, too."

"I don't care. Caitlyn loves raisins." Carefully, Barnabas lifted the chicken onto his lap. "Aren't you real, Caitlyn?" He dug in his pocket for a raisin, then held out his hand palm up. After a moment, he popped the raisin in his mouth. "She's too upset to eat right now."

Maya couldn't help hearing, but she didn't have to listen. Instead, she thought about Ms. M.

Poltergeists in the library. Really?

Chances were it was just kids messing up the shelves. But with Ms. M around, you never knew. Anything seemed possible.

For a few seconds, Maya smiled. Then her dad pulled into the driveway and her smile, kind of like a ghost, faded away.

Once out of their booster seats, the boys bolted for the house.

"I'm going to fiddle around with the car for a while before your mother gets home." Her father pointed at his 1965 red Mustang. He'd inherited it from Maya's grandfather

and drove it to vintage car shows almost every month.

He slung an arm around Maya's shoulder and pulled her close. "You okay, Maya-papaya?"

That's highly debatable, she thought. Out loud she said, "Yes."

In the kitchen, a trail of spilled cheddar popcorn led toward the family room, where the boys were watching *Space Rangers*, their favorite cartoon. Maya took a banana and a raspberry juice box and retreated upstairs.

With a sigh, she put down her snacks and threw herself on the bed.

Her A+ mobile of the solar system hung by the window. Right by her desk stood the cool antique globe her parents bought when her Wisconsin map won "Most Accurate" in the third-grade geography fair.

On her desk sat the pile of flash cards she'd made to study for the spelling bee. A word on one side. A definition on the other.

If she'd won, she'd be studying them right now. And making new cards with even harder words, like *conscientious* and *disciplined*. Words that once described her.

If she'd won, the trophy would be downstairs in the rec room right under her dad's INSURANCE SALESMAN OF THE YEAR plaque and her mom's framed OFFICER OF THE MONTH certificate.

But she wasn't studying. And there was no trophy downstairs.

Maya stood up, marched to her desk, and started tearing up note cards.

One after another. Into smaller and smaller pieces that fluttered onto the blue carpet like snowflakes. When she was finished, she lay down on the floor and spread out her arms and legs. As if she were making a snow angel.

She was still lying there when her mother knocked.

"I came up here to see if you needed sympathy." Her mother stared down at her with a bemused expression. "But it looks like what you really need is a vacuum."

Scraps of note cards clung to Maya's shirt sleeves and her skirt as she slowly got to her feet. "Sorry. I'll clean up."

"Yes," her mother said, sitting down on the end of the bed. "You will. After we talk for a bit."

Her mother patted the space beside her. Maya sat. She leaned until her forehead bumped against her mother's shoulder. "I studied really hard, Mom. You know I did. I guess I'm just not good at spelling anymore."

Her mother took one of Maya's hands. "Remember when I didn't pass the physical fitness exam at the police academy? I couldn't do thirty sit-ups or run three hundred meters in under a minute. Did I quit? No, I joined a gym. Next time I took it, I beat almost everybody."

"Next time." Maya sighed. "That's what Dad said."

"I know you're upset. And I don't blame you. But I also know you're not a quitter, all right?"

"I guess," Maya said. Though was that really true? She'd retired from gymnastics when she was six, because hanging upside down gave her headaches. She'd dropped out of karate last year because all that yelling—"Hi-ya!"—hurt her ears.

Spelling was different. Spelling mattered.

Spelling was something she loved. And she thought spelling loved her back.

Until today.

Her mother stood up. "Leave this mess for now. We have to eat dinner fast so we can get to B and V's soccer game."

"Am I going to have to sit on the sidelines and pretend to watch Caitlyn and Maximus?"

Her mother said, "Well, sweetie, while you're at it, why not pretend to have a good time?"

Chapter 7
A Possible Explanation

Ants.

A colony of red and blue ants swarming a colossal cookie.

That's what a first-grade soccer game looks like, Maya decided.

Standing on the sidelines next to Fernando's dad, her father yelled, "Spread out, Rockets!"

From the center of the swarm, Barnabas waved and charged in the wrong direction.

Maya and her mother sat in canvas folding chairs a little farther back from the action.

"What in the world is Victor doing?" Her mother squinted toward midfield, where Maya's other brother knelt, drawing in the dirt with his finger. "He's about to get run over." She called, "Come on, V! Get up and help your team!"

Still on his knees, Victor gazed placidly at the ball as it rolled past, the swarm following closely behind.

Quirky little brothers. They weren't all that bad, Maya decided, when viewed from a safe distance. They were almost entertaining. Diverting, even. For a little while.

"Mama, can I go over to the playground? You can see me from here."

"Take Caitlyn with you." Her mother flashed a teasing grin and mimed handing her the chicken. "B says she loves the swings."

The hubbub faded away behind Maya as she headed down the hill toward the mostly deserted playground. There were a couple of little kids over by the monkey bars with their parents. A girl pogo-sticking on the basketball court. A kid in a blue hoodie gripped the merry-go-round with one hand while another kid in a pointy hat pushed him round and round.

Pointy hat?

Maya hurried closer.

Unbelievable! "Ms. M. What are you—"

"Oh, hello, Maya dear. I'll be with you

in a second. Daniel and I are conducting an experiment."

When the merry-go-round slowed to a stop, Daniel staggered into the sand. "Wow! I thought I was going to fly off!"

"Exactly. That's centrifugal force at work. The force you use by holding on is *centripetal*."

"So cool, Ms. M. I get it now. Thanks."

Daniel happily wobbled off in the direction of the drinking fountain, allowing Maya to finish her question. "What are you doing here?"

"It's my new home away from home. For now." Ms. M pointed to a neat pile under the big sycamore tree. A small roller suitcase. A cauldron. A tightly rolled sleeping bag. And curled next to the sleeping bag, blinking in the golden evening light, Ms. M's black cat, Onyx. "Sadie's playhouse is unavailable, and Jess's father just returned from his series of road games, and I didn't want to impose."

"So, um." Maya took a deep breath. "Sadie and Jess know you're back?"

"Goodness, let's hope not. That way we can surprise them at school tomorrow." Ms. M took Maya's hand. "Come say hi to Onyx. And don't worry about the bird. She's too big for him to chase."

Bird? Maya peered at the nearest tree. It didn't have that many leaves, much less a blue jay or a crow.

"Right at your feet." Ms. M gestured toward Maya's rainbow high-top sneakers. "That handsome Rhode Island Red. Such a hardy breed. Caitlyn, isn't that right?"

"You see her?" asked Maya.

"Witches are often familiar with what appears not to be there." Ms. M crouched down and moved her lips, but, as far as Maya could tell, no sound came out.

"The words are invisible, too," Ms. M explained without being asked. "I told her that Onyx wouldn't hurt her, but she still seemed nervous. So she's on her way back to the game to watch Barnabas. Now, come along."

The witch's hand was so warm! Maya let herself be led over to where Onyx uncurled, stretched, and then nudged Maya, asking to be petted.

She rubbed Onyx under his chin, feeling his deep purr of pleasure, as Ms. M ladled some . . . well, something out of the cauldron.

"Have you eaten?" asked the witch. "There's plenty."

It looked like stew but acted more like lava,

inching slowly toward the edge of the plate. Maya retreated a bit. "I'm fine. Thank you, though."

Ms. M dug in, pausing now and then to give Onyx a taste on a special cat spoon.

A cheer erupted uphill. As improbable as it seemed, one of the teams must have scored. Maybe her brothers would finally win a game. Her brothers, who didn't even care about soccer. Who spent every practice goofing around. Mom and Dad would probably take them all out for ice cream to celebrate.

And all she got was a lousy red ribbon.

"I—" Maya hesitated, and then forced the six words out quickly. "I lost the spelling bee today." She slowed for the two words that weighed more than the others: "Sadie won."

Ms. M wiped the cat spoon on her black

smock dress, stuck the spoon in her pocket, and turned to Maya. "I know what that's like. Ethel beat me in a smelling bee when we were in pungency class together at the Supernatural School. It wasn't entirely my fault. I confused lime and grapefruit because one of the other students came into the room riding a unicorn, and I was distracted."

Maya managed a smile. "Too bad I didn't have a unicorn to distract Sadie."

"Did I say unicorn? I meant unicycle. In any event, I wasn't at my best that day, and Ethel won."

"How did you feel?" Maya asked.

"Disappointed. Embarrassed."

"Yes! Me, too." Maya sat up straighter. "That's why I'm never going to spell again."

"Good for you. Lots of famous people gave up. You know the story of Jake and the Beanstalk."

"You mean Jack, don't you?"

"No, no. Jack bravely climbed the beanstalk and had adventures. Jake was afraid of heights, so he and his mother just sold beans."

Maya was dubious. "I've never heard that story. Are you just making it up, or is it real?"

"That depends on what you mean by *real*, dear. Would you mind holding Onyx for a moment? I need to get our bed ready." Ms. M picked up Onyx and poured him into Maya's lap. Then she said, "Tomorrow will be a big day. That library poltergeist is very active. You'll never guess where I found *The Adventures of Captain Underpants*. In the pirate section."

Maya stroked Onyx as she said, "You know, Ms. M, that could make sense to a first grader who was just trying to be helpful. And, anyway, kids move things around all the time." She scratched Onyx between the ears. "It's no big deal."

"Yes, that's a possible explanation, but not a compelling one."

Just then Maya heard her mother call, "Myyyyyy-a!"

"I have to go." She lifted Onyx and set him down gently in the grass. He didn't even wake up.

"Of course. But spare me one more moment." In a single flourish, the witch unrolled the bright blue sleeping bag. "Now, open this up right at the top, and hold it at the end of the tube slide."

"Why?"

Without answering, the witch snatched Onyx and scampered up the steps to the very top of the slide. "Ready, dear?"

Maya unzipped the bag a little. She held it as Ms. M had directed. "I think so."

"Here I come! Wheeeeeeeee!"

Maya braced herself but really didn't need to. The witch slid into the sleeping bag like a hand into a glove.

SHOOSSSSH.

"Are you all right?" Maya asked.

The witch's head popped right up. "Better than all right. Cozy as can be."

"Are you really going to sleep right here on the ground?"

The witch adjusted her hat. "I've been a camper all my life. Ethel and I had the loveliest little tent. She made the best mugwort s'mores."

"Myyyyyya!"

"That's your mother," said the witch. "Your little brothers' team won at last. Now run along, dear. Onyx and I are fine. I'll see you tomorrow in the haunted library."

As Maya started back up to the soccer field, she half turned and saw Onyx slither out of the sleeping bag and begin to groom his ruffled fur.

Myyyyya!

Chapter 8
Bookhenge

Usually Maya loved getting to school early so she could talk to Sadie and Jess before the bell rang. This morning she approached her cubby warily. It wasn't that she didn't want to see her friends. She just didn't know what she would say to them. Especially to Sadie.

She tightened the straps on her backpack

and took a deep breath, as if she were about to begin an arduous hike.

There they were, sitting side by side on the floor in the hall, Sadie in her favorite red T-shirt that said BIRD BRAIN over a cartoon of an owl writing math equations on a chalkboard. And Jess in the black-and-white-striped sweater that made her look like a small but determined referee.

"Hey," Maya began, but before she could say anything else, Sadie shot to her feet. "Maya! I'm so glad you're here. My parents found my trophy!"

Maya took a deep breath. "I'm really sorry. I didn't mean to break it."

"*You* broke it?" Sadie looked confused. "Mr. Frederick said the antenna came off, and he glued it back on. I just wish"—she gripped Maya's hand, hard—"he had thrown the whole thing in the trash!"

Maya couldn't help smiling. A little. *Take that, bee.*

"That way my parents never would have found it in my backpack," Sadie continued. "But they did. And now they're all excited. They even called my grandmother, and she's coming for the district spelling bee. All the way from St. Louis!" Sadie finished with a wail.

"And she's bringing a video camera," Jess added.

"And she knows how to post to YouTube." Sadie groaned and let her head drop onto Maya's shoulder. "So there's going to be a movie of me clutching the microphone, stuttering, passing out. It'll go viral."

Jess gave Sadie a friendly nudge. "You won't lose. The only person who knows how to spell more words than you is Maya."

"That's why I need to leave the country. So Maya can take my place. And win."

Maya patted Sadie's hair. "You'll be fine."

Sadie raised her head and shook it so hard

that her ponytail swished against Maya's cheek. "I won't. The only way I'll be fine is if you are up on that stage, and I am on a plane to Bolivia."

"Green anacondas live in Bolivia," Maya said. "I watched a show about them on the nature channel. They can be deadly."

"I'll take my chances," Sadie said. "What's really deadly is me trying to spell *anaconda*. Aren't there at least five *A*'s in that word?"

Mr. Frederick appeared in the classroom doorway. "Maya, I just received an interesting email from the substitute librarian. It seems that you and the other two musketeers are wanted in the library for a special research project."

Uh-oh, thought Maya. *Here we go*. She jumped to her feet. "We started it yesterday.

She said she might need more help."

"She promised not to keep you for long, and"—Mr. Frederick raised his eyebrows in confusion or amusement, Maya wasn't sure which—"she offered me donuts if I let the three of you out of class. I told her that bribery was not required. The students of Room 142 are always happy to pitch in."

As they made their way toward the library, Sadie asked, frowning, "What kind of research project is it? Why does she need all of us?"

"You'll see," Maya said. "It's a surprise."

She let Sadie and Jess walk into the library ahead of her. Over their shoulders she could see the witch peering intently at one of the computers lined up along the north wall like so many friendly robots.

"Ms. M!" Jess called, forgetting to use her library voice.

Sadie turned toward Maya with a huge grin. "*Now* everything makes sense."

The witch—her pointy hat resting beside her on the table—lifted her gaze from the

screen and smiled her typically warm smile. "Girls, it's so lovely to see you again. Come see what I found on BOOgle."

"You mean Google," said Jess. She and Sadie took turns giving Ms. M a hug.

"No, dear, BOOgle. It's a special search engine devoted to paranormal activities and, of course, recipes. Ethel loved their Ghostly Goulash."

Sadie moved toward the computer. "Mr. Frederick said something about a research project. Is it about Ethel?"

"Not this time." Ms. M motioned the girls closer to the computer. "Take a look."

The screen showed three photographs: one of a white wall with a painting askew; another of a shattered teacup; and another of an orange cat with eyes narrowed and ears laid back.

"Shocking, aren't they?" said Ms. M. "These are verified photographs of a poltergeist at work."

Sadie and Jess looked at Maya.

"*Poltergeist* is German for 'noisy ghost,'" Maya explained. "Ms. M thinks the library is haunted."

"Yes!" Jess pumped her fist. "We get to be ghostbusters."

"Let's catch the poltergeist and take it to the district bee," said Sadie. "Everyone will run out of the auditorium screaming!"

Maya pointed at the computer screen. "C'mon, Ms. M. Someone was dusting and moved that painting. Anybody can drop a teacup, and probably a dog scared that cat."

"I wouldn't be so sure." The witch grabbed her hat by the tip and deposited it on top of her head. "Follow me."

She led them over to the blue table in the corner. Books were scattered across it. A few leaned against the windowsill. Some lay open, looking half-read and abandoned. Some sprawled facedown, as if they'd fainted.

Maya smoothed the wrinkled pages of *A Single Shard* and closed it gently. "I wish *people* would take better care of books." For emphasis, she repeated. "*People.* As in living human beings."

Ms. M waved a hand at the mess. "I made this display of Newbery Medal winners yesterday for a fifth-grade teacher, and I wasn't surprised this morning to find it in this condition. Poltergeist energy is destructive. But it's what's under the table that's really puzzling." She pulled out a chair and crouched down.

On the carpet beneath the table was . . . well, what, exactly? Some kind of square structure made from picture books. At the center of the square sat a yellow cushion from the reading corner.

"That's why I was consulting BOOgle," explained the witch. "Normally poltergeists don't build. But they *are* tricksters. This one may just be trying to throw us off track."

"Off what track?" asked Sadie.

"The track it doesn't want us to be on," said Ms. M.

"It *is* mysterious," Jess admitted. "Like Stonehenge."

"Except," Maya pointed out, even though no one seemed to be listening, "Stonehenge was built in England out of massive rocks about five thousand years ago."

"Well, maybe this is Bookhenge," Jess ventured.

"Why would a noisy ghost make something like that?" Sadie knelt next to Ms. M. "I mean, what would be the point?"

"Hard to say why spirits do anything. I do know they are attracted to turmoil. If a poltergeist is present, it usually means someone in the house—or in this case, the school—is upset."

Maya knew libraries were generally quiet

places, but all of a sudden the library got even quieter. As if it were holding its breath.

Finally Sadie blurted, "Oh, great. I'm upset about the spelling bee. And now the library is haunted."

Maya didn't say anything. She still didn't believe in any ghost. She really and truly didn't. What she did believe in was being a good librarian's assistant. She plucked the books one by one from under the table and stacked them in a neat pile.

Jess raised her eyebrows. "Is Sadie's poltergeist going to like that?"

Maya plopped the cushion on top of the pile and stood up. "Sadie doesn't have a poltergeist. There is no poltergeist, okay?"

Except even as she said the words, in a tiny

corner of her mind, she started to wonder. Curious things *had* been happening. Unusual things. And Sadie wasn't the only one who was upset about the spelling bee.

What if there *was* a poltergeist in the library? And what if it wasn't Sadie's poltergeist? What if it was hers?

Chapter 9

Emerald on the Inside

After lunch, on their way out to recess, the girls stopped by their cubbies.

Jess held up a fat, dark pink flower with layers of petals. "Where did this come from?"

"It's a zinnia," Maya said. "My mom grows them in our backyard."

"Okay, but what's it doing in my cubby?"

Maya sighed. "I bet it's from Maximus. Victor's imaginary friend. He has a crush on you."

"Victor does?" Jess twirled the flower beneath her nose, closed her eyes, and sniffed. "Or Maximus?"

"Exactly," said Maya.

Outside on the playground, they bypassed the mayhem of freeze tag and red rover and drifted toward the tetherball court. Sadie and Jess positioned themselves to play, but Maya hung back. She thought she saw Ms. M standing under the GROW IT. STUDY IT. EAT IT. banner at the entrance to the schoolyard garden. For sure that was the witch's pointy hat, but what she wearing over her black dress? A long plaid shirt with . . . straw sticking out of the sleeves?

"I am so doomed!" Sadie shouted, bringing Maya's attention back to the game. Sadie punched the ball and spelled, "D-o-o-m-e-d."

"No, you are so weird!" Jess caught the ball and swung it toward Sadie with one hand while holding on to the pink flower with the other. "W-i-e-r-d."

E-i, Maya mentally corrected her. *Weird.* She glanced toward the garden again. "I'll be right back."

She zipped past some third-grade girls who were doing double Dutch at what looked like supersonic speed, wove through a maze of frozen freeze-tag players, and, nearing the entrance to the garden, called out, "Ms. M!"

When the witch turned and waved, a dusty shower of straw rained from her sleeve. "What perfect timing," she said cheerfully as Maya approached. "You can help me fill the bird feeders."

"I'd love to." Up close Ms. M's outfit was even stranger. The plaid shirt swooshed around her ankles when she moved. Her sleeves bulged with packed straw. "You look like a scarecrow,"

Maya said finally. "Kind of, anyway."

"Yes, I always dress for the occasion." Ms. M beamed. Then she added, "It's not that I have anything personal against crows. But they do tend to hog all the sunflower seeds, and those are Ethel's favorite." A soft rustling sounded as she bent down, hefted a bag of birdseed onto her shoulder, and straightened. "All right, dear, follow me!"

In the center of the garden, three feeders hung from a metal pole by loops of strong wire. The first one Ms. M reached for had a slanted roof and three wooden walls. It looked like a tiny rustic cabin in midair. She lifted it down and held it steady while Maya scooped.

"Fill it to the brim," Ms. M advised her.

"Birds need to put on weight for the cold weather ahead."

"Do you really think Ethel might be around?" Maya asked as she pulled the cork from the top of the next feeder, which was made from a mayonnaise jar turned upside down and glued to a blue-and-white china saucer.

"Most yellow warblers are on their way south by now, but Ethel's always tardy. If she is in the area, I want to make sure she has plenty to eat. I can't bear to think of her going hungry."

"You're a good friend."

"You are, too, dear. You and Jess and Sadie."

"Except," Maya began, and then stopped.

Stretched up on tippy-toe to hang the feeder back on the hook, Ms. M turned her

head to look at Maya. "Except?"

"Except I'm jealous of Sadie." There. She'd said it. Out loud. She kept her eyes down and concentrated on scooping seed into the last feeder, a clear plastic tube dotted with holes and metal perches.

Ms. M didn't answer right away. When Maya snuck a peek at her, she was stroking her chin thoughtfully.

"You know," the witch said at last, "when I went to Supernatural School, we learned to regulate our emotions. My friend Cliona Crowe was so good at it that I turned green with envy. Our teacher thought it was hilarious. The color didn't fade for weeks."

"So jealousy doesn't last forever." Maya sighed. "That's a relief."

"Yes. After a lot of practice, I could turn from emerald to fern to mint fairly quickly."

Maya examined the skin on her arm. It was as brown as always. "Maybe I'm emerald on the inside?"

"You're a lovely color, dear. Inside and out."

"Even if I still feel—"

Suddenly the witch pursed her lips and emitted a series of shrill whistles. A half dozen small brown birds assembled on the garden fence, like diners waiting for tables at a restaurant. They ruffled their feathers and chirped in response.

Ms. M turned to Maya. "They're getting impatient, but I told them we're just about finished here. Let's clean up."

After returning the birdseed to the supply shed, Ms. M pulled a plastic garbage bag from her pocket. Maya held the bag open while the witch collected stray food wrappers, squashed cups, and other odds and ends that didn't belong in the garden. She deposited the trash in the bag and wiped her hands on her plaid shirt.

Just then, from across the playground, Sadie bellowed, "Hopeless! H-o—oh, NO!"

Maya turned to see the tetherball, now detached from its rope, shooting across the playground. It bounced a few times, slowed

to a roll, and came to rest at
Ms. M's feet.

"Wow," said Maya.

"Wow, indeed," said the witch.

Jess waved and shouted, "How about
a little help over here!"

Ms. M picked up the ball, held it over the
toe of her pointy shoe, and gave a tremendous
kick. The tetherball rose in a graceful arc.
And kept rising. Everyone on the playground
stopped what they were doing and watched.

Just when it seemed like the ball was going
to vanish into the troposphere, it started
down, plummeting like a meteor until it
landed in Jess's outstretched hands.

The whole playground cheered. Ms. M
stepped forward and bowed.

"For a while, I was the place-kicker for the Sheboygan Shamans," she explained to Maya. "Muscle memory. The body never forgets."

An hour later, Maya was halfway through a work sheet of two-digit multiplication problems when Mr. Frederick called her, Sadie, and Jess up to his desk.

"I just got another email from the substitute librarian. All in caps. She'd like to see the three of you for a minute. You may go, but this is the last time, okay?"

Running in the halls wasn't allowed, but Jess was walking so fast that Maya had to trot to keep up. "I hope it's about the ghost!" Jess grabbed Maya's arm and tugged her along.

"Do you think the poltergeist made the

tetherball come loose?" Sadie asked.

Maya blinked hard to keep from rolling her eyes. "I think," she said, "that your pounding it like the Incredible Hulk was the relevant factor."

"Relevant," Sadie repeated. Her face turned as pale as, well, a ghost. "Does that have two *L*'s and three *E*'s?"

As they entered the library, Ms. M called out, "Over here, girls."

The witch was crouched beside the blue table, almost beneath it.

"Is everything okay?" Maya asked.

"Once was a little out of the ordinary, but twice? Highly unusual."

Jess stared and said, "Awesome!"

Sadie blinked and said, "Oh no."

Maya looked. Leaned and peered. Squatted and scrutinized.

There was no denying it: the same picture books arranged in a square, the same yellow cushion.

Bookhenge was back.

Chapter 10
Not a Game for Babies

There had to be a logical explanation. Someone must have snuck in and rebuilt it. Someone or—

As if reading Maya's mind, Ms. M said, "I'm certain it wasn't there when I returned from the garden. It must have appeared during first-grade story time. My finest performance of 'The Sleeping Sorceress' yet." The witch beamed and straightened her hat. "It's a wonderful story. About a lovely young witch who wakes up from a hundred-year nap when—"

"The prince kisses her," Jess finished.

"No," said Ms. M. "When she has to use the bathroom. A hundred years is a long time to hold it."

Sadie twisted the end of her ponytail around her fingers. "Okay, so we know the poltergeist is still here. How are we going to get rid of it?" She turned toward Maya. "I think the only solution is for you to take my place at the spelling bee."

"And that's the only solution because . . . ?"

Sadie continued. "Because I'm the one

attracting the ghost, right? I'm the one who's upset. But if I don't have to be in the spelling bee, then I won't be upset anymore, and then just like that"—Sadie snapped her fingers— "no more poltergeist."

"We don't know for sure what summoned this particular spirit," said Ms. M, her brown eyes meeting Maya's. "Or who."

Maya ducked the witch's gaze and pretended to tie her shoe. Why had she ever

admitted to being jealous? She snuck a peek under the top of her sock. Her skin wasn't green, thank goodness. Though inside she still felt a little ferny.

Jess clapped her hands so loudly that Maya almost toppled over. "Well, I don't care who attracted the ghost, as long as we catch it!"

Maya regained her balance enough to ask, "How are we supposed to do that? It's not a butterfly. We can't just scoop it into a net."

"I thought you didn't believe in noisy ghosts." Jess crossed her arms over her chest and looked smug.

"I don't. But if I did, I'm sure catching one would be a complicated procedure. Right, Ms. M?"

"Actually, before you arrived, my new

friend from BOOgle gave me instructions for a ceremony to rid any space of negative energy." The witch rubbed her hands together as if she were about to sit down to a delicious meal. "I don't quite have all the materials for the ritual, but we can make adjustments. Let's get started."

They followed the witch over to the checkout desk, where she opened the deep bottom drawer, pulled out her dusty black bag, and began digging through it.

"Normally we'd use incense, candles, salt, and a special silver chalice. So I looked in the staff lounge, and voilà!" She took a slightly

stained, white "World's Coolest Teacher" mug out of the bag and set it on the desk. "It looks silvery in the right light."

Next came a package of fruit-scented markers.

"Let me guess," said Maya. "That's our incense?"

The witch nodded. "I believe the orange and the grape will be the most effective. They're quite aromatic."

A-r-o-

Maya forced herself to stop and focus on the small pile of mini flashlights Ms. M plunked down next to the markers. "Candles don't meet the school district's fire safety code, but these will do nicely. And of course I always carry Wistful Witches' Low-Sodium

Sorcery Salt with me." She placed the salt shaker next to the flashlights and closed her bag. "Finally—and this is important—we meet at the grove of yew trees at midnight."

"Except," said Maya, "that I have to be in bed by nine."

Jess nodded, and Sadie added, "Sometimes earlier."

"Hmmm." The witch tapped her chin and appeared to be thinking. Then she said, "Well, it's almost midnight somewhere in the world. We'll pretend we're there. Now let's all sit on the floor."

"But—" Before Maya could finish objecting, Jess, already sprawled on the rug, grabbed her hand and tugged.

From the other side, Sadie nudged her.

"Just remember, Maya, if this doesn't work, you're going to the bee, and I'm going to Bolivia."

Ms. M sat across from Maya. She patted the carpet beside her. "Sadie, sit here, please.

Facing Jess." Once all four of them had settled into place, the witch rubbed her hands together briskly and gave Maya a big smile. "Ready?"

"And this is going to . . . ?" Maya let the question hang there.

"Rid the library of negative energy," Ms. M said.

"By sitting here staring at each other?"

The witch held up her hands. "Palms together to begin."

Maya sighed and pressed her palms against Ms. M's.

Whoa! The witch's hands were so warm!

"All right then." Ms. M moved slowly at first to demonstrate. "Hands on your thighs, then hands together, then crisscross with your partner." Speeding up as the girls followed her lead, she began to chant. "Peas porridge hot, peas porridge cold, peas porridge in the pot—"

Maya stopped midclap. "Wait a minute. That's a nursery rhyme, not a spell."

"Who says it's not both?" Ms. M asked.

Jess made a face. "Maya's right. How is playing a game for babies and talking about peas going to help us get rid of a ghost?"

When Ms. M held up her hands again, Maya felt heat radiating from the witch's palms. "You didn't let me finish the chant," said Ms. M. "I'll start again." She cleared her throat noisily. "Peas porridge hot, peas porridge cold, peas porridge in the pot, nine days old. Poltergeist, poltergeist, get out of here. Scram, vamoose, take a hike, disappear!"

Suddenly the lights flickered. The computer screens went blank before booting up again with a whir and a deep, mysterious bell-tower tone.

"Excellent!" Ms. M cackled. "We've got that pesky ghost out of hiding. Faster, girls, faster!"

So they went faster! Slapping their thighs and clapping and crisscrossing. And all the while the witch kept chanting. "Scram, vamoose, take a hike, disappear!"

Maya was panting, breathlessly trying to keep up with Ms. M, when the air conditioner turned itself on! She shivered as a blast of cold air hit her back.

The lights flickered again and went off. Then on again. Then off. Maya grimaced and shut her eyes tight. Her thighs ached from all the pounding. Her hands stung from all the clapping. Ms. M's chant turned into a torrent of words that swirled into meaningless syllables. Through the torrent, Maya heard the creak of the library door. Was someone— or something—on its way out?

She opened her eyes just as the lights stopped flickering and gave up, plunging the room into darkness. And that's when someone or something whispered hoarsely, "Maya?"

"EEEEEEEEEEEEEEEEEEEYIKES!!!!"

Sadie's and Jess's screams echoed Maya's. Enough light seeped in from the hallway through the open door for Maya to see . . .

Barnabas.

"Hey, what are you guys doing?" he said. "I thought you were supposed to be quiet in a library."

Chapter 11

Imaginary Eggs

Maya leaned against the nearest table for support, her heart hammering in her ears like rain on a roof. "Barnabas! What are you doing here?"

"I don't have to tell you." Her little brother scowled. "And neither does Caitlyn."

"I hope we didn't frighten her." Ms. M

stepped forward. "She really is a lovely bird. Do you mind if I pet her?"

"Go ahead. Scratch the back of her neck. She likes that best."

Barnabas held out his apparently empty hands, and the witch moved her gnarled fingers rhythmically in the air above them. She murmured, "So nice to see you again, my friend."

"So this is our ghost?" Jess said, sounding more than a little annoyed. "An imaginary chicken? But what about the lights? And the computers? And the air conditioner?"

"I'll put in a call to the maintenance man to check the circuit breakers," the witch said.

Barnabas scolded Jess. "Just because you can't see Caitlyn doesn't mean she's imaginary." He pointed across the room. "I built her a nest under that table over there, but someone keeps messing it up."

"Correction," Sadie said. "Our ghost is a first grader."

"Six-year-old boys are similar to poltergeists," said the witch. "Especially the noisy part." She took a step back and said in a hushed tone, "Caitlyn seems to have fallen asleep. Shall we put her in her nest?"

"I'm glad it wasn't me and my turmoil attracting the ghost," Sadie told Maya as they all trooped over to the blue table.

Or me and mine, Maya thought.

Barnabas leaned over the walls of Bookhenge and lowered Caitlyn onto the yellow cushion. He mumbled something Maya couldn't hear, stood up straight, and grinned. "She says she likes it! Can she stay here tonight with you, Ms. M? She'll lay an egg for sure!"

"Yum." Jess rubbed her stomach. "Imaginary eggs go great with imaginary bacon."

"Of course she can." The witch smiled her usual warm, crooked smile. "Caitlyn and I will get along just fine." She turned to Maya. "It's supposed to rain, so I was planning to sleep here, anyway. And if Caitlyn still doesn't feel comfortable around Onyx, she can stay in my black bag. She won't mind at all. Since the platypus left to find a pond, she'll have plenty of space."

Barnabas rocked back and forth on his toes. "Wait till James and Fernando see Caitlyn's egg. That'll show them."

They won't see anything! Because she's not *real!* That's what Maya started to say. But something about the look on her brother's face stopped her. He was so excited! She could tell how much he wanted—no, needed—his plan to work.

But what would happen tomorrow when he brought his friends into the library and showed them the empty nest? Correction:

the plain old yellow cushion with nothing on it. She hated to think about what his face would look like then.

After school, when their mother pulled up in the blue van, Maya let Barnabas and Victor climb in first. She followed, making sure her brothers' seat belts were buckled before settling into the backseat.

"How is everyone?" their mother asked. "Any interesting news?"

Maya waited for Barnabas to start talking about Caitlyn, but he just stared silently out the window, so she volunteered. "I worked on a research project with the substitute librarian. She's . . . unconventional. So it was interesting."

"That's my girl." Their mother glanced appreciatively at Maya in the rearview mirror. "I knew you wouldn't let that spelling bee keep you down."

"Maximus is going to ask Jess to his birthday party," Victor reported.

"I'm sure she'll be thrilled," said Maya.

"He's almost seven," Victor added. "And he's very mature for his age."

Their mother slowed for a yellow light. "What about you, B? Did you have a good day?"

"Yeah."

"Are you tired, honey? You can take a nap before dinner."

"I'm not tired!" Barnabas squirmed in his booster seat. "I'm thinking."

"Well, there's nothing wrong with that," their mother said, turning on the radio to the jazz station she liked.

Maya draped herself over the seat and, under the cover of a saxophone riff, said quietly to Barnabas, "Don't worry about

Caitlyn. Ms. M will take good care of her."

"Will she know that Caitlyn likes banana slices for her bedtime snack?" Barnabas asked.

"Probably," Maya assured him. "She knows a lot about a lot of things."

But did she know how to get an imaginary chicken to lay a real egg? Probably not.

When they pulled into the driveway, there was Dad, polishing the already sparkling hood of his Mustang. Victor jumped down from the van, ran over and climbed into the front seat of the car, and went "*Vroommm, vroommm.*" Mom started that way, too, and their father opened his arms to wrap her in a hug.

Maya followed Barnabas as he clattered through the front door, dragging his Spider-Man backpack behind him, and bounded into the kitchen.

She could almost hear his friends laughing at him. Again.

"How about a juice box?" Maya said, sounding cheerier than she felt.

Barnabas shook his head. "Milk, please."

"Even better. Chocolate milk with lots of syrup. Just the way you like it."

When Maya opened the refrigerator door, it was as if a light came on inside her head, too. With a glance back to check if Barnabas was looking, she slipped something into her pocket, then quickly grabbed the milk and chocolate syrup and set them on the table along with a glass and a spoon. "Can you make your own chocolate milk? I just remembered

I have to take something to Ms. M."

Her little brother grinned. "Make sure you tell her about the banana. Three slices sprinkled with sugar right before bed."

Maya laughed. "Got it."

"Thanks!" Barnabas drizzled a puddle of chocolate syrup onto the spoon and popped it into his mouth.

She zoomed out the front door, almost

crashing into her mother, who was on her way in.

"Everything okay?" her mother asked. "Or should I call the fire department?"

"Do you think Daddy would take me back to school? There's something I forgot to do. For the research project. It will only take a minute."

"Any excuse to drive that car, if you ask me. Just be back by dinnertime."

A few minutes later, she was cruising with her dad. He had his window down and the radio turned up.

"Can we go a little faster, please? I want to catch the substitute librarian before she, um, leaves." A tiny lie was easier than trying to explain to her father that the substitute librarian was a witch spending the night in the library with a cat named Onyx.

"This is a '65 Mustang," her father said. "A classic. People want a good look at this beauty."

When they finally pulled into the circular pickup zone, Maya shot out of the car,

through the double doors, past a couple of students coming out of Robot League and a surprised Mr. Lopez, the after-school piano teacher. She burst into the library and found Ms. M sitting at her cluttered desk. The witch looked up and said calmly, "Hello, dear. I was just thinking about you."

Maya reached into her pocket and showed Ms. M what she had brought. "Okay?"

Ms. M beamed. "You read my mind. It's perfect."

Chapter 12
Thanks for the Help

The next morning when Maya's dad dropped her and her brothers off at school, Barnabas started toward the library, but Maya stopped him. "Go get your so-called friends. I'll find Sadie and Jess. Meet us by Bookhenge, I mean, the nest in three minutes, okay?"

"I'll tell Maximus," said Victor. "If Jess is

going to be there, he'll want to—"

"Fine," said Maya.

Sadie and Jess were huddled together by the cubbies. As Maya approached, Jess held out a flower. "Maximus strikes again."

"I wonder where Victor found this." Maya examined the bright yellow daisy. "It didn't

come from our yard. And when did he put it in your cubby? I've been with him all morning."

"Maybe he didn't put it in my cubby." Jess tucked the flower behind her ear and grinned. "Maybe Maximus did."

"Well, you can ask Maximus because he's waiting for us in the library right now," Maya said. "Along with an imaginary chicken who is as invisible as he is, some real first graders, and a diminutive witch." She linked arms with her two best friends. "Let's go."

"Diminutive." Sadie swallowed hard. "D-i- . . . um . . . -m- . . . ugh."

As soon as she opened the library door, Maya heard Barnabas's voice. She followed it over to the little crowd clustered around the blue table. There were her brothers and

Ms. M. There were James and Fernando.

From the look on Barnabas's face, she knew things weren't going well.

"It does *so* prove something, you guys." Barnabas stomped his foot for emphasis.

Ms. M gave the girls a welcoming smile, then reached across Fernando and patted Barnabas's arm. "That is a first-rate, Grade A egg. Caitlyn should be very proud."

"She is proud. Look." Barnabas glanced down at his outstretched hands. "She's smiling."

"What's the big deal?" James pointed. "Anybody could have put that there."

Maya peered under the table at the nest Barnabas had built. Right in the middle of the yellow cushion, just as Maya had planned, was the smooth brown egg.

"Anyway," said Fernando, "why would an imaginary chicken lay a real egg?"

Barnabas looked at his sister. Maya looked at Ms. M, who stepped closer so they were standing arm-to-arm. There was the witch's usual warmth, her familiar cinnamon smell.

"Except she's not imaginary," Maya said firmly. "Caitlyn's right there." She turned toward Barnabas. "Can I pet her? I know how much she likes that." Barnabas held up his hands, and Maya stroked the air above them. "Good chicken," she murmured. "Good Caitlyn."

Jess handed Victor her flower. "Hold this while I pet Caitlyn, okay?"

Sadie moved closer. "Then me, please. She is so cute."

"This is weird," said Fernando. And then, after a moment, "Can I pet her next?"

"Then Maximus," said Victor, peeping shyly at Jess.

James shook his head. "Okay. Fine. I give up. She's real. And lays eggs. Now can we just play soccer at recess?"

"It's Caitlyn's turn to be goalie," Barnabas said.

"All right, my dears." Ms. M clapped her hands. "The bell's about to ring. You need to get to class, and I need to get ready for my nine-o'clock performance of 'Little Bo Sweep,' the rags-to-riches story of an enterprising witch who owns a discount broom outlet in Sausalito. Barnabas, why don't we give Caitlyn's egg to your sister to look after for the day?"

The other boys charged for the door like a herd of small ponies, but Barnabas hung back just an instant to give Maya a hug. Then he was gone, too.

Jess twirled her daisy, which was starting to droop. "C'mon, I want to stop at the water fountain and give this flower a drink."

"You guys go ahead," Maya told her friends. "I'll be right there."

After Jess and Sadie left, Maya picked up the egg and gently placed it inside her padded lunch sack, between her sandwich and her package of mini chocolate-chip cookies.

"Caitlyn wanted me to tell you thanks for the help," said Ms. M. "She's starting to molt,

and all her egg-laying energy is going toward growing new feathers. She did want you to have these, though." The witch reached into her familiar black bag and brought out three reddish-brown feathers.

Maya took the feathers and smoothed them with two fingers. She held them up to the sunlight streaming in from the tall north window and watched their tawny color change to carob, then mocha, and back again.

"Tell Caitlyn thanks," said Maya as she stuck the feathers in her pocket.

The witch's eyes twinkled. "You can tell her yourself, dear. Next time you see her."

Chapter 13

One Codfish and Two Sharks

The school day was almost over. Maya handed in her Spanish work sheet to Mr. Frederick and sat back down. While she waited for everyone else to finish up, she arranged the three feathers side by side on her desk. Wherever Ms. M had gotten them, they were beautiful. Almost pretty enough to make her forget

about Monday's limp red second-place ribbon. Almost. But not quite.

On the front blackboard, under "Classroom News," it still said "Congratulations, Sadie, School Spelling Bee Champ!" in slightly smudged blue chalk. Reading it was like chopping an onion—the words stung Maya's eyes. She turned away and gazed out the window.

And that's when she saw it. Saw *them*.

Two small yellow birds, one with slightly darker feathers than the other, perched on one of the feeders. Suddenly a big bully of a blue jay swooped in, and the yellow pair took off out of sight.

Maya stared at the spot where they had been, willing them to return. It felt as if she had imagined them, as if they had never been there. But they *had*. She was sure of it.

She couldn't wait to tell Ms. M!

When the bell finally rang, she gathered her things from her cubby and raced out to the pickup circle. As her father opened the minivan door, she said, "Can I run and talk to the substitute librarian? I'll be back in a minute."

Barnabas pushed past her and climbed into his seat. "Don't take forever. Caitlyn's starving. She needs a snack."

Victor followed his twin. "Maximus, too. He wants french fries."

"Tell you what, boys," their father said. "Mama's working the late shift tonight, so she's home taking a nap. How about we go to Lucky Burger and then swing back and pick up your sister. We'll order you a strawberry shake, Maya. With rainbow sprinkles. Sound good?"

"Sounds perfect." She leaned into the van, kissed her father's cheek, and took off toward the library.

Maya burst through the door. "Ms. M?" The witch wasn't at the circulation desk or by the computers or on the story carpet.

"Over here, dear."

Ms. M sat at a study table next to Sadie. Between them lay a dictionary, a thesaurus, and a stack of index cards. "Ms. M is showing me her guaranteed super-secret method for winning the spelling bee!" Sadie sounded more cheerful than she had in days.

The witch swept her hand across the dictionary and the thesaurus as she said, "She'll have both of these memorized in no time, thanks to techniques handed down through the ages and known only to a few. Now then, Sadie." Ms. M opened the dictionary to a random page. "Spelling is often very logical. For instance, look at *secretary*. That word knows how to keep a secret. *Secret* plus *ary*. See?"

"Yes, but that's just one word out of a million." Sadie began to look nervous again.

The witch flipped to a new page. "Here's another example. *Necessary* has one C, but two S's, as in 'It is necessary for a shirt to have one collar but two sleeves.'"

Panic rising in her eyes, Sadie turned to Maya. "What does a shirt have to do with spelling?"

"Would you prefer one codfish and two

sharks?" said Ms. M. "Or one cobra and two sidewinders—"

"No! No snakes! The shirt is fine."

"Now with a word like *obsidian*, you're in luck. Listen and learn: Ophelia, Babette, Sabrina, Iris, Daphne, Irene, Athena, Nancy. The first letters of all of their names spell *obsidian*!"

"Who are those people?"

"My teammates in the Dark Moon Ladies' Dodgeball League. Really fun gals. I'll introduce you sometime."

"Okay," Sadie said. "But what if they don't ask me to spell *obsidian* or *codfish* or *sleeve* or whatever? What if they ask me to spell something like *pharaoh* or *convalesce*?"

The witch frowned. She took off her hat and scratched her head. Finally, she said, "Let's just hope that doesn't happen."

With a groan and then a *thunk*, Sadie banged her head down on the table. Turning her face toward Maya, she said, "I guess I better start packing for Bolivia."

"It's a lovely country." Ms. M began tidying up the table, stacking the books and notecards into a neat pile. "There are one hundred forty-eight bird species there. The blue-throated macaw is on my wish list."

"Um, Ms. M, speaking of birds." Maya stepped forward. "I think I might have seen Ethel at the feeder."

The witch rushed to the window so fast that her chair teetered. Maya and Sadie joined her, and the three of them peered out at the garden. After a moment, Ms. M shook her head and said, "Only chickadees out there now. She must have moved on."

"She'll be back," Maya assured her. Even if it might not be true, she hated to hear Ms. M sound so sad. Then she added, "She was with a friend. They looked kind of alike, only one was yellower."

"Male warblers are more brightly colored

than females," said Sadie, her eyes widening. "Hey, maybe Ethel has a boyfriend!"

"I assumed she'd find a mate." The witch leaned against the windowsill, her back toward the glass. "Ethel's always been popular." She sighed. "They could be on their way to Florida or Mexico together. Ethel loves the beach."

Maya reached for Ms. M's hand. "Or maybe she wants to say good-bye to you before she leaves. So when she comes back, you can ask her where she's going and visit her there."

"You're right, dear. Let's look on the bright side." The witch let go of Maya's hand and stood up straighter. "The world is full of possibilities."

"And after you visit Ethel in Florida," said Sadie, "you and Maya and Jess can come visit me in Bolivia, and we can—"

"This is *ridiculous*!" Maya blurted out before she could stop herself. And now that Sadie and Ms. M were looking right at her, she had to go on. "Sadie, you're not going anywhere. Except to my house. To study. My dad will call your dad. You can stay for dinner, and we can study more after that. I'll help you. Okay?"

Sadie looked unconvinced. "You'd really do that?"

Maya was emphatic. "I a-b-s-o-l-u-t-e-l-y would. Besides, if I'm going to win next year's spelling bee, I need to study, too."

Chapter 14
C-e-l-e-b-r-a-t-e

On the day of the district spelling bee, the auditorium was, appropriately enough, buzzing. The seats were filled with parents and grandparents and kids. Some wore T-shirts with logos like BRANSON SPELLERS and WILSON WORD WARRIORS. Everyone waited excitedly to cheer on the twenty-four participants now filing onto the stage.

"Excuse me." Sadie's grandmother leaned in between Maya and Ms. M. "Would you mind taking off your hat? It's blocking my shot."

"Not at all." The witch set her black pointy hat on the floor by her feet. Then she reached into her black bag and pulled out an identical smaller version. It was shorter, but just as pointy. She confided to Maya, "I don't feel like myself without one."

On Maya's other side, Jess scooted forward in her seat and squinted. "What's Sadie holding?"

"I gave her one of Caitlyn's feathers," Maya replied. "For good luck."

Ms. M said, "And I told her to remember that a crocodile in gingham went to kindergarten in a limousine." When Maya and Jess stared at her blankly, she added, "Those are four very tricky nouns."

Maya felt a tap on her shoulder. It was Sadie's mom. "I just want to thank you for all your help," she said. "Sadie was so sure you'd win the school spelling bee, and then when she won . . . well. Let's just say she's had a very difficult couple of weeks."

Maya thought of all the things she could

say, like *Me, too* or *Tell me about it*. She decided on, "You're welcome."

Sadie's dad pointed toward the stage. "Looks like we're starting!" Maya swiveled back around to see a man in a suit stand up from the row of judges and walk to the microphone. He thanked everyone for coming and laid out the simple rules. "Spell correctly and you get to stay onstage. Miss a word and you're out. Good luck, spellers!"

A tall girl from Wells Elementary went first.

"Wistful," said the pronouncer.

Maya spelled the word quickly in her mind. For sure she

knew what it meant—longing for something with regret. She glanced at the gleaming winner's trophy rising up like a skyscraper from a table at the side of the stage. *Regret*, she thought. *No kidding.*

The tall girl spelled *wistful* correctly. A boy from Morrison Academy made his way through *interference*. But the next two spellers left the stage after *amphibian* and *etiquette*. The words seemed to hover in the air, waiting for Maya to spell them. Silently, she did, and then watched them disappear.

Finally it was Sadie's turn. She gripped the microphone as if it were the only thing holding her upright.

Maya knew that all Sadie wanted was not to miss on the first round, with her

grandmother filming. With her parents, her friends, and hundreds of strangers watching.

Ms. M grabbed Maya's hand and squeezed. Jess leaned so far forward that she looked as if she were about to catapult out of her chair. Maya held her breath. *C'mon, c'mon, c'mon.*

"Poltergeist," said the pronouncer.

In the lobby after it was all over, Sadie ran up and wrapped Maya and Jess in a hug.

"Sixth place!" Maya beamed with pride. "Out of twenty-four. Good for you. A highly respectable showing."

Sadie laughed. "Yeah, now I'm glad I'm not in Bolivia." She turned to hug Ms. M while her grandmother circled them, still filming.

"Poltergeist," said Jess, shaking her head slowly and grinning.

"I know!" Sadie held up Caitlyn's feather. "Did you work some magic on this, Ms. M? It really did give me good luck."

"You and Maya put in a lot of hours of studying. But a little magic never hurts. Oh, I almost forgot." The witch reached into her black bag. "I have something for you." She pulled out a slightly wilted but fragrant yellow rose. "From Maximus."

"Hey!" said Jess. "Does that mean Victor has a crush on Sadie now?"

Maya shrugged, but the witch shook her head. "No, Victor is smitten with Desiree, a girl in his class. At least that's what Maximus told me."

Sadie's dad came over and kissed his daughter on the head. "Everybody ready? We're all going someplace special for lunch to c-e-l-e-b-r-a-t-e."

"Let me get a group photo first," said Sadie's grandmother. "Girls, Ms. M, squeeze together."

As Maya tucked herself between Jess and Ms. M, her gaze traveled across the room to where the winner of the bee, a smiling girl from Bethune Elementary, stood clutching her trophy and talking to a reporter and a cameraman from Channel 4 News. The trophy was almost as tall as she was.

Next year, Maya couldn't help thinking. *Next year that's me.*

Behind the winner, the second-place speller sat slumped on a bench by the wall.

His head drooped. His little trophy lay on its side at his feet.

"Look this way, Maya!" Sadie's grandmother chirped. "Everyone smile!" She took the picture and examined the screen. "Beautiful."

"Would you mind emailing that to me?" asked Ms. M. "My address is onyxmama@ hocuspocus.com. I'll print it out and frame it the moment I get home tonight."

"You mean you're leaving?" Sadie moaned, and Jess added, "Again?"

Maya's heart sank.

"Now that Mrs. Gardiner has recovered, my services are no longer required in the library. Also, I got a call from the physical education teacher at the Supernatural

School. It seems she's heard strange noises coming from the equipment room. And—" Ms. M motioned for them to come closer. She looked left and then right before leaning in to whisper, "Someone or something let all the air out of the gooches."

"What are gooches?" Jess whispered back.

"You need gooches to play snoodle, of course." The witch straightened. "It sounds like spontaneous psychic activity to me. She needs my help."

"But you can't leave," Maya objected. "What if Ethel shows up at the feeder again?"

"She and her mate are likely halfway to Miami by now. They won't be up this way again until spring. Though one never knows with Ethel. If they showed up at my house,

I wouldn't be surprised." The witch clasped Maya's hand. "You'll keep the feeders filled here, won't you? Just in case?"

"Sure. I promise." Over the witch's shoulder, Maya saw the second-place speller sit up enough to kick his trophy out into the walkway, where a man almost stepped on it.

"We're going to get the car," Sadie's mom called. "Meet us out front." Sadie and Jess started toward the door, but Maya hesitated. "I'll be right back," she said to Ms. M.

The witch's eyes twinkled warmly as she released Maya's hand. "I'll wait here."

Maya strode over, picked up the trophy, and held it out to the boy. "You dropped this."

"Take it if you want it." The boy gestured without looking up. "It's all yours."

"No, thanks. I've got my own second-place prize." Maya set the trophy beside him on the bench. "You did great, though. Those words were tough. *Stelliferous*? Were they kidding?"

The boy flashed a wan smile. "Doesn't matter. I'm never spelling again."

"I know how you feel."

"I seriously doubt it."

"Seriously. I do. But it gets better after a while. B-e-l-e-i-v-e me."

At that the boy raised his head. Slightly. "It's i-e-v-e. *I* before *E* except after *C*."

Maya broke into a grin. "See?" She turned around and headed over to rejoin Ms. M.

"Okay," she told the witch. "I'm ready."

"As am I," said Ms. M. "If I leave now, I'll be home in time to pick up supper from the Tasty

Toad. Onyx loves their tuna melts." She patted her bulging black bag. "Don't you, my dear?"

From inside the bag came a muffled "meow."

"I'm really going to miss you," said Maya.

"I'm really going to miss you, too. But I thought I'd leave in a dramatic way. Something memorable."

"What do you mean?"

"I'll disappear. Here one moment"—the witch snapped her fingers—"and gone the next."

"Um, isn't that what you usually do? Sadie and Jess said that you just—"

"Yes, but this time with smoke and sparkle.

Perhaps you'd better put on your sunglasses!" The witch hoisted her black bag onto her shoulder. She raised her arms overhead, shut her eyes, and chanted softly.

Maya didn't even let herself blink. A few seconds passed. Then a few more.

Ms. M stopped chanting and opened her eyes. "Drat. I must have gotten my *abras* mixed up with my *cadabras*."

Just then Sadie popped her head back into the lobby. "Are you coming or what? I'm starved."

"On our way," Maya called. She turned to say, "Let's go, Ms. M." She paused. "Ms. M?"

Maya was alone. The witch was gone.

Outside the auditorium, under a suddenly cloudy sky, Maya found her two friends waiting by the curb.

"Where's Ms. M?" Jess asked. "I thought she was with you."

"She was," Maya said. "And then she wasn't."

Fat raindrops began to fall.

Sadie pointed. "Wait. Is that her?"

Across the parking lot, what looked like a tall black hat moved through the crowd until . . . it opened into an umbrella.

"No," said Jess. "It's not. It's just a normal person."

"Looks like she did it again," said Maya. Then she added, "*Poof.*"

"I bet she'll be back." Sadie looked decisive. "She kind of migrates, you know?"

Maya smiled. "Yeah. She kind of does."

Sadie's dad's SUV pulled up just as it began to pour. Her grandma rolled down the back window. "Girls! Quick, before you're soaked!"

Maya held out her hands. One for Jess. One for Sadie.

Together, they ran.

What's Haunting You?

Noisy German Ghost or Invisible Chicken

Unsure whether your mysterious visitor is poltergeist or poultry? Take this BOOgle quiz and find out!

1. How do you wake up in the morning?

    A. Ducking a flying alarm clock.

    B. A loud *Bok bok BOK* in my ear.

    C. My mom wakes me up.

2. If you can't sleep at night, it's because . . .

    A. Something went *bump*.

    B. Something went *squawk*.

    C. I sleep like a log every night.

3. Under your bed you find . . .

    A. The math book I left on the kitchen table just a minute ago.

    B. Straw, hay, twigs, and a stash of seeds.

    C. Dirty socks, dust bunnies, candy wrappers. The usual stuff.

4. Don't you want to sit in your favorite chair?

    A. Sure, but it's levitating up near the ceiling. Who can jump that high?

    B. I have a strange feeling that it's already occupied. And by *strange feeling* I mean—ouch!—something is pecking my—ouch!

    C. I would love to, thanks.

5. How do you like your eggs?

    A. *Not* coming ninety miles an hour straight for my head!

    B. *Not* on my pillow or in my sock drawer.

    C. Scrambled with a side of hash browns.

6. Or would you like cereal for breakfast?

    A. That would be great, but the milk is probably in the dishwasher. Again.

    B. I'll try Raisin Br— Hey, who ate all the raisins?

    C. Oatmeal and brown sugar for me, please. *Yum.*

7. **When your best friend calls . . .**

    A. I can't hear over the thumping and moaning on the stairs.

    B. I can't hear because my cat is growling and hissing at something clucking under the table.

    C. "Hi. What's up?"

8. **How do you get to school?**

    A. Dad drives me when he can find his keys.

    B. I walk really fast because I'm afraid the sky is falling.

    C. I take the bus.

9. What's your favorite way to spend a quiet evening at home?

    A. I'm sorry, could you repeat that? SO MUCH THUMPING.

    B. Pulling feathers out of my hair.

    C. Watching movies with the fam.

10. Have you been upset about anything lately?

    A. Are you kidding? Would you like to dodge speeding eggs?

    B. I'm okay except for the invisible chicken poop on my left shoe.

    C. Me? I'm great. I'm a fountain of positive energy.

AAAAAAAAAAA—
CHOOOooooo !!!!!!!

11. Gesundheit! That was a big sneeze. I hope you're not catching a cold!

    A. I blame the pepper grinder hovering under my nose.

    B. I am, but it's nothing a nice hot bowl of chicken noodle soup won't— Ouch! Ouch! Ouch!

    C. Nah, I have allergies. They're always bad this time of year.

Answer Key:

Mostly A's: Your naughty trickster is a poltergeist. Though surprisingly quiet in libraries (how thoughtful!), poltergeists often make a big fuss by thumping on walls and moving furniture around—sometimes up! They like to throw objects—*duck!*—and make adults shout inappropriate words by hiding their wallets in the litter box. Poltergeists tend to be attracted to moody children and teens. In fact some experts believe they aren't spirits at all, but rather examples of psychokinesis in which all evidence of the "haunting" is caused by an irritable young person's mind. So the next time you are having a bad day at school and your pencil case shoots across your desk, don't worry. Either you're in the presence of a noisy ghost or you are one.

Mostly B's: Chances are, your invisible guest is feathered. And hungry. Shut the cat in a back room for a bit, crouch down with a handful of raisins, and speak softly. That's the way to tame the savage beak! Once the two of you get to know each other, your friend may feel comfortable enough to share her eggs. Unless, of course, she is a he—a rooster, not a hen. In which case, go ahead and throw your alarm clock right out the window, or invite a poltergeist to do it for you.

Mostly C's: There are no signs of anything out of the ordinary in your house. You go to school, talk to your friends, come home and play, but none of these activities are rudely interrupted by thumps or obnoxious pecking. There is nothing wrong with that! Though sometimes your daily life can get a little dull. May I suggest taking up a hobby? What about painting or quilting? Or even writing ghost stories! You never know what your active imagination might conjure up.

Fun with Mnemonics
by Ms. M

Hi, everybody!

I was digging in my black bag for my binoculars and guess what I found instead? A cool spelling tip. Remember Ophelia, Babette, Sabrina, Iris, Daphne, Irene, Athena, and Nancy from my dodgeball team? (Fun gals!) Remember how the first letters of all their names put together spelled *obsidian*, and I promised Sadie that would help her always get that word right?

Using my friends' names like that is an example of a mnemonic device or, for short, a mnemonic. That's a real mouthful, isn't it? And it's pronounced like this— nuh-MON-ic (a handy rhyme for supersonic, if you're writing a poem).

You might want to come up with a mnemonic to help you remember how to spell *mnemonic*. Here's mine: <u>M</u>y <u>n</u>ose <u>e</u>jects <u>m</u>ucus <u>o</u>n <u>N</u>ancy's <u>i</u>cky <u>c</u>arpet. Who could forget that? Certainly not Nancy. And now not you, either!

Mnemonics are named after Mnemosyne (nuh-MOSS-uh-nee), the Greek goddess of memory. You can bet that none of the other goddesses ever saw Mnemosyne staring at a shopping list at the Mount Olympus Food Mart. She

MNEMOSYNE

didn't need one; she never forgot anything.

Once you start thinking of mnemonics, they're like poltergeists. They're everywhere. And they're not just good for spelling. They're great for remembering anything.

For example, you might be familiar with one of Ethel's favorite mnemonics, ROY G. BIV, which helped her remember the colors of the rainbow—<u>R</u>ed, <u>O</u>range, <u>Y</u>ellow, <u>G</u>reen, <u>B</u>lue, <u>I</u>ndigo, <u>V</u>iolet. Ethel liked it so much that she named her pet bat Roy G. Biv. Whenever I see a rainbow, I don't think of a pot of gold but of Roy, who would come when Ethel called (but only in the dark).

Mnemonics belong in everybody's backpack. Have fun with them! In fact, let's have some fun together. Check out the names of

ROY G. BIV

the planets, from the sun outward: <u>M</u>ercury, <u>V</u>enus, <u>E</u>arth, <u>M</u>ars, <u>J</u>upiter, <u>S</u>aturn, <u>U</u>ranus, <u>N</u>eptune, and <u>P</u>luto. How about we think up a mnemonic to help us remember them in the right order?

I'll start us out—<u>M</u>ost <u>v</u>egetarians <u>e</u>at <u>m</u>any . . .

Finish and write me back. I can't wait to see what you come up with!

Bye for now,

Ms. M